The life of Lido Pepperman

The life of Lido Pepperman

albert klassen

The life of Lido Pepperman

Publisher: DEE ELL PUBLISHING

ISBN: 978-1-7782809-1-7

Further information: albertklassen@icloud.com

chapter one

the flautist played in the park
notes deep and melancholy
the air smelling of burning leaves

I'm still lost you know
in this little world I made up
shut the door please
the breeze
is blowing in
and it's ugly
and it's cold
pass the coat please
freedom is sucking the warmth out of me
as the answers are flying away

blind eyes
deaf ears
dumb tongues

oh look - the sky is red
and the glory of the lord
not lost
was I dead
not even for a few minutes and then
brought back like a lazarus
no
it seems that I am still lying in my bed

the army of canvasses are arrayed against me
it's not me
I'm not the enemy
why are they so stacked
forcing me out of my window
out onto the ledge
I fear the ledge
so high
and I could fall - and then
I'll become the next Saviour and save you all from
hell
bless me father
curse me father
in pretense I come to you
with cold ambition
like the wind

shut the door
the window has a screen
saved my life
I wonder about all of that
and all those friends
they left me or
shunned me or
did I drive them all away with my crazy ideas
my penchant for nonsense
makes me think twice
or thrice
tried to fit in but
somehow
they all got up and left

then I went to the bank
on the way they were standing at the movie theatre
said hi and was happy to see them
there was warmth in my heart
they said you're not welcome
go away
pulling my coat tight around me I shuffled away
glancing back
they waved me on

at the bank the teller smiled at me as she counted
out my money
that was not unkind
I smiled back

after all these years and still not famous
come here little kitty
you are at least my friend
and then of course there's alice
she got lost in the fog last year
and I'm still waiting
or is she out for lunch
she used to bring me treats
she used to smile
come here kitty
but she's coming back
I feel it
she had things to do
the fog's been gone a long time now

the darkness never seemed to be so dark
it's stark
can't even see sometimes
thank god for the lamp
it stands beside my bed on a shelf

my disguise is still intact
I'm fooling myself
it's always been easy to fool me
a blessing from god
in the tall grass I hide
and my glasses are the wrong prescription
but who cares
no one
in blind disarray we stagger

together
here all alone
except I have a kitty
love my kitty
here kitty come here kitty

am I losing something
perhaps I'm out of touch
maybe I really am lost
can't tell anymore

she came in through the door in pink panties and a
disorder or two
whispering about the monsters
cursing her birth
with long legs
looking at me with those far away eyes
piercing blue
then asking me if I'd read to kill a mockingbird
I loved that book - she said
in my mind I was like - ya you're mad like the dog
but I smiled

the knock on the door was deafening
she opened it up and in popped a freddy come lately
always some brash know it all to tell me how to live
you know if
she brushed him off with a curt - what
and - get out
and - now

I smiled again
some people have a knack
a way of getting their point across without wasting a
lot of energy or words
hey pink panties what's up
again - fuck off
she turned on the t.v. and lit a cigarette - one of
those ultra thin ones
the chinese like them
very stylish and fashionable

why do strange women come to visit me
I gave them no invitation
I don't know them
don't think I've seen them before
I'm not attractive
I'm not rich
I'm not famous

I sit at my table eating cream of wheat porridge and
toast
is that all you have
no
well
eggs and sausage in the fridge
forget it I'll get something
she slammed the door as she left
why
I paged through the latest vogue - it's the september
issue

and it's disappointing - dam

where is alice
she has an unfinished painting sitting in the storage
room
I know she's coming back
she needs to finish the painting
unless she's dead somewhere
she never calls and
her phone seems to be not in service

the darkness is closing in on me
my head hurts
I wonder if I'm dying
this is it I know it
where is that bright light
where is my jesus
quit toying with me
let's get it over with
I open my eyes and I see the light but it's my lamp
still alive and I'm disappointed and then
relieved

why such detachment as if
life was an otherworldly experience
everything becomes ordinary and still - unusual
a contradiction
words all collide and become metaphors that confuse
and befuddle
nothing is everything

and staring into the emptiness past my window I
shudder
trying to grasp some version of reality that makes
sense
inside a scream is forming and edward's painting
comes to mind
he knew

now - nobody knows anything
bereft of wisdom and empty of truth
a floundering humanity sitting at the table of
satisfaction
dropping crumbs laced with the poison of arrogance

in the background the music plays always
a soundtrack of life and living
looking back I shudder again as memories come
flooding back
triggered by the music
deep sadness
all those regrets - could have been something
and accomplished so much but I was terrified and
confused
now my loneliness overwhelms me
I cower under the blankets
the door opens and in saunters miss pink panties
she sits on the recliner in front of the t.v. and eats a
piece of pizza
want one she offers
I climb out of bed - ya

thanks
together we watch a rerun of I love Lucy
she laughs and giggles the whole time
I watch her more than the show
really a very gorgeous woman
seen her before - but where
time never stands still
the show must go on and I love Lucy is over
she lights another cigarette and offers me one
I don't smoke anymore but take one
she lights me up
ah-h-h
I feel cool
cigarettes are so sexy
after a couple of drags I'm calm
thanks
ya

she takes off her clothes and lies in the bed making
eye contact with me
I approach cautiously

it's dark when I wake up - midnight the clock on the
wall says
she's gone
it's just me and the cat
the t.v. is still on and the music too
a cacophony of conflicting sounds
like my life
messing around was always such fun but after

doubts and questions
was I good enough
did I satisfy her
did I have bad breath
was I too flabby
dam I hate sex - it exposes my fears and anxiety
can't just enjoy it
no always a complete analysis is in order
and that goes on for days
sometimes weeks
sometimes years
it never ends
it's not worth it

lovers come and go
questions remain unanswered
feelings battered and bruised collapse into the centre
as the might of human thought comes to its knees
unmasked- love is still a stranger
beating us senseless till in a stupor we babble
incoherently
our strength diminished
our humanity extinguished
our dreams shattered

chapter two

the sun is like a precocious god
illuminating and exposing
using power to abuse
the rays demand answers
get up
do something
make something of yourself
set goals
accomplish some great work of art or write an
amazing song
endless pressure
come on come on
my laziness is exposed and I cower under the covers
even here she pushes her agenda

I hate the sun
I hate summer
I dream of winter and night and rainy days
vancouver is my solace
my refuge
rain is king here and the sun his servant

wake up the teacher shouted
what's wrong with you
don't you sleep at night
are you a misfit or a retard
why is your homework not done
why are you so lazy
why - why - why

knock knock knock... a timid knock on the door
come in
sir I've got your grocery delivery
put it on the floor thank you
ok
bye
bye
the cat goes over to the three bags and sniffs
no kitty no food for you there
dam I forgot
I pour the kitty some food in her bowl and top up
the water
kitty I forgot about you
she eats her food and looks up at me and meows
nice kitty

good kitty
I pet her - she arches her back and purrs
why do some people not like cats
they're so loving and so little work
I love that they have their own agenda
not like a dog who's always in your face
demanding attention just like some people
some people are like cats
others like dogs
I like cat people

I take the broom and sweep the suite - a two
bedroom
one bedroom is my studio and the other for my bed
then a big room with an attached kitchen and a
separate bathroom
and a large storage room
1000 sq.ft. - big enough for me
I like small spaces
I can handle small spaces
I can keep them clean
there's a deck - 8X10 with three chairs and a table
and a barbecue - electric
I live like a king here on floor number 19
overlooking english bay

how much room do we need
how much is waste
is it about power
traditionally the big man lived in the big house and

so on
we all want to be big men
we want
and want
and want
nothing is ever good enough
nothing is ever enough
give me more
and more
and more
dam
my couch is a futon from ikea
I always leave it in couch mode
I sit down
the kitty is all curled up on the other end
so cute
so peaceful
I love cats
I click on the t.v. to watch the news
another guy shot up a joint killing many people
another earthquake killing many people
another little war killing many people
that's a cheerful way to start the day
hallelujah and whatever
why do I bother to watch all this stuff
why am I addicted to it all and can't help myself
who am I
who are we
what are we

I've been toying with the idea of getting a tattoo
why I don't know
maybe I want to look dangerous and cool
and interesting
who wants to be boring
oh hi so and so - how are you
good good
anything new
well funny you should ask
got a tattoo yesterday and it
hurts
let's see it
here
wow so cool
any tattoo is cool
you can't go wrong with a tattoo
that settles it - I'm getting a tattoo

reach out your hand
I need you in this heartbreak land
so many times it has been broken - my heart
to tell the story - where would I start
there were queens and drummers
there were hussies and bummers
they came and they left
leaving me scarred and bereft
that's when I was looking for the sun
cause I was cold and - done

I sigh as the sadness washes over me

and go to where I always go
to bed
to my dreams where I think of spaceships and utopia
a land where I'm happy and free
from all my cares and woes
who will rescue me now
who will care
who can open up this window and show me
something good
something wonderful
the kitty licks my face
I stroke her
she is my sunshine here in this darkness
a darkness I invite and then shun
conflicted man that I am
full of contradiction and remorse
drifting

I wake up to the sound of the t.v.
and the smell of cigarettes
pink panties is sitting on the recliner smoking a
cigarette and drinking a beer
I sit up
she glances at me
I go to the bathroom
then make cream of wheat and toast and sit down at
the table and read the latest georgia straight
she wanders over and makes herself a couple pieces of
toast
she takes my spoon and tastes the cream of wheat

can I have some
help yourself
she sits at the table with me eating cream of wheat
toast drinking a beer and smoking
this woman is mental I think to myself
and who is she and where did she come from and why
is she so assertive
and why me
some people really have some nerve
and me I just accept it - why
no self image
no self respect
I am timid
shy
terrified of life
so that means people come and roll over me
wish I could be a real man but that's not going to
happen
you either got it or you don't and I don't
it is what it is
but why

pink goes to the bathroom and then to my bed
she lays down and wraps herself up in the comforter
the kitty snuggles up next to her
it's like it's always been this way
the man
his woman
and his cat
I light up one of her cigarettes and blow smoke at

the light
dam
it feels good
domestic bliss
I laugh
pink stirs and looks at me - then turns over

reality morphs into surrealism
dreams and yearnings force the imagination to
conjure up sweet nothings
smiles dance upon the faces of the children
we play and make up where we are
and where we've been
as magic touches us so deep
inside where so much has died
where amelia cried as beatrice sighed
and belief gave way to doubt and strategy
as the debaters dressed up in jet black tuxes and
stuck their noses in the air
calling us all losers and killing our fantasies

down on the ground we groaned as the jesters danced
all around us
poking sticks at us and laughing uproariously
it's all so helter skelter

god took a chance on mankind but we let him down
building temples and towers
as we tried to reach him
each in their own way

generations inventing their own interpretation of the
divine
while angles flitted here and there throwing
moonbeams
and holding up the son of man for all to see
worship and obey they chanted as mary turned her
head away
tears running down her face
she put a record on the turntable but there was no
power
then jesus lifted his hand and the record played
and we danced as he smiled and stroked his mother's
head
all was well in the kingdom of god

chapter three

yesterday - paul said it well
trouble wasn't invented when we were young
living in our own cacoon
protected by our mothers and fathers - at least for
most of us
some suffered early and the scars remain
never to heal despite all the self help books and
therapy
and the drugs mask the pain but only temporarily
the suffering continues
the faces show the pain

I make myself some kraft macaroni and cheese
it's become a ritual - like communion
it's comforting and i've been eating it for 30 plus

years
I mix in fried onions green onions corn sausages and
relish
pink panties awakens to the smell of food and joins
me at the table
we polish it all her and I
she goes to the bathroom and has a shower and then
she's gone
who is this woman
looks like she's about 40
such a familiar face and why did she come to my
condo
was she sent here by someone - maybe even god
life can be so mysterious and weird sometimes
and that's not really a bad thing
I like her coming and going - it's interesting
I clean up and put the dishes in the dishwasher
have a shower and then go to bed
her perfume is on my pillow

episcopal leanings were not my thing
wearing ripped up jeans were also not my thing
listening to george carlin was my thing
it's a shame he's gone
he put everything into perspective
taught me about important things
clued me in to the value of bitterness and crass
observations
it all went so well with my sunday school lessons
church was so boring

it just about killed me
the same old thing over and over again
the boring sermons
the pretentious preachers and elders pontificating
and acting all holy
even a kid can see through all that
what the hell

I should really lock my door but I have a hang up
about it
if I need to escape I don't want to fumble with the
dead bolt
and who's going to attack me on the 19'th floor
well I guess anyone
people come unannounced thru my door all the time
I could get robbed or killed anytime really
but still - I won't lock my door
maybe I'm just rebellious
lock your door
you must lock your door
no I won't

who's going to come in and kill me
I just don't believe someone will do it
they might kill someone in the next building but it
won't be me
and they'll want to break down the door like in the
movies
if the door is open the thrill is gone
they try my door - hey joey this one's open

well forget it man ain't gonna be nothing good in
there
everyone knows that if there's something valuable the
door is locked
see that's the way criminals talk
that's how they think
so the door stays open and you know what
everyone likes it like that
it's like come on in you're welcome

I drift off and then wake up
kitty is licking my hand
hi kitty - I pet her and she purrs
what a nice little friend
what a good girl
you're such a good girl
I get up and check her food and water
no problem there
I clean her litter - it's the scoopable kind
works real well
kitty comes and eats some food
she's a happy little cat

the door opens and in walks johnny
hey
what's up
you got ten bucks I can borrow
I reach in my pocket and give him 2 fives
thanks man
no problem

he's gone

from pay check to pay check
heaven help us if there's an emergency
life is a struggle
most of us are one emergency away from throwing in
the towel
constant pressure
a life not worth living
when I was young I could hardly wait to be old
all that freedom
do what you want
no one there to tell you what to do
now - I live in a prison
everyone tells me what to do
I can't do what I want
scared to death
what happened
this is not how I imagined it would be
but this is how my teachers warned me it would be
did I think they were lying
or making it up to scare me
don't know what I was thinking
I was young
innocent
stupid
naive

the vesper bells are ringing
the chanting has started

the monks are walking slowly in a procession
long robes swishing as they walk
a mindless activity designed to reach the father
sacred ritual that hearkens back
barefeet to symbolize the holiness

sinful human nature always causing us to do bad
things
stuffing our bellies full of food and drink
indulging our appetite for destruction and mayhem
as the guitar blasts forth a cacophony of distortion
venting our rage on the stage
baring our teeth and
promising violent overtures

a knock on the door
come in
I have a package for a mr.pepperman
that's me sir
sign here please
thanks
thanks
bye
bye
finally my paint supplies
I rip open the package and take out the valuable
contents
some new brushes - very nice
some acrylic paint - mostly I needed titanium white
for someone as depressed as I it's funny

I use a lot of white in my paintings
I allow myself a smile
true happiness is getting new brushes and more paint
move over night
here comes the light
but never fear
soon we'll be shifting gear
and all will be dark again

I fear happiness
I'm scared that something very bad will happen if I
rejoice too much
don't want to tip off the keepers of the universe that
I am happy sometimes
they desire that I suffer and am sad
if I show some joy then a double dose of tragedy will
follow and my despair
it will drive me deeper into the dark hole
and if I go deep enough there is no escape and I'm
finished
so I respect the universe and don't tempt fate
keep the joy to a minimum and the lips tight
let the brushes and the knife do all the talking
silence human
don't pretend that you matter
you know you don't
you are a nothing
an outcast
worthy of pain and suffering
my lot in life

my reward for being born

I go to my studio which is small - 10 X 10 but it
works for me
organize my materials and brushes
now to get inspired
haven't painted for 2 weeks
in a funk
depressed and no ideas
need a jolt to the system
johnny goes out and buys me magazines from the
used store sometimes
I call him
johnny can you get me some magazines
he's coming over
maybe I'll get some ideas
I never look at other art
I build on my own ideas - evolve on my own
picasso said to steal and I do but not from artists
at least not directly
art confuses
I never know what to paint
I only do abstract
can't stand painting something realistically
I make up stuff and disobey any rules
I am a rule breaker
my art is my rebellion against everything
dam this and dam that
and forget about it please

my friend gudrun a tall blonde german is my agent
she has the connections and takes half of the price
she sells to galleries to individuals on the internet -
everywhere
this woman is something
born in berlin 5 1 years ago and now living in berlin
and new york
never stands still and knows her stuff
she calls me all the time encouraging me
where would I be without her
she has an assistant - a guy named alfredo
he hangs out with me for days sometime
we drink beer and eat pizza and tell jokes
love that guy
then gudrun is looking for him
alfredo where are you
get your ass in gear I need you here and there
and poor alfredo gets all nervous and off he goes-
hitler's calling he says
these people are my family
they keep me alive

I fill the tub and have a bath complete with bubbles
I play music from my ipod which sits in a cradle in
my bose player
the doors are playing - people are strange
and people really can be strange
we're all different but as long as we respect each
other and love each other
well - maybe we can make this world a better place

I'm not an optimistic person but I do hope for
something good
god knows I'm not doing my part hiding away and
complaining
I hope for better people
stronger
courageous
mature

chapter four

it's one o'clock in the morning and I'm painting
again
music is playing on my Bose and I'm lost
lost in an abstract world of imagination and wonder
I paint
stand back
sit on my chair and analyse
what to do next
splash paint all over the canvass
got to try something different
have to correct my waywardness
back in line
just as in life where the masters tell us to get back in
line
conform and be one of the followers

don't colour outside the lines
except here there are no rules or
am I deluding myself
maybe there are rules and without knowing it
I am obeying the masters of art and design
I perceive randomness but
is it true
who's pulling my strings behind these mortal
constraints
who's installing blinders on my eyes
is this a yoke I feel

it's time for bed
I sink into the nothingness

I wake up to the smell of perfume and the t.v.
pink panties is lying beside me in the bed
johnny is watching t.v. drinking beer and eating
nachos
johnny what's the time
10:00 in the a.m.
I pull the covers over my head and keep on sleeping
I wake up again and nothing has changed
pink panties is still beside me with kitty curled up by
her head
kitty likes pink panties
johnny is still drinking beer and eating nachos
what's the time Johnny
1:00
I get up and go to the bathroom and have a shower

while I'm in there pink panties comes in and takes a
wee
morning
morning
pink is back in bed
kitty rubs against me meowing
I pick her up and pet her
what's up kitty how are you good girl
I check her food and water - all ok
I sit down beside johnny who has a giant stack of
magazines sitting on the floor in front of him
good work johnny boy how much do I owe you
nothing but we're even
right on bro
I page through a few of them - looks good these are
old this one's 1972
johnny gets me a beer and we sit and watch t.v. and
eat nachos
pink joins us after some time
johnny gets her a beer and we sit there together
watching t.v.
pink lights up and lights up johnny
I decline

the door opens and in comes frank
hey bud
hey
frank gets a beer and sits on the recliner
he says no to nachos but lights up
I might as well be smoking too for all the smoke in

here
I go and open the window
frank steals my seat
I think he likes pink
he's chatting her up
shut the fuck up
ok ok he retreats back to the recliner
I laugh
pink is a tough babe

the door opens and in comes joshua with a click of
the heels
looks like a party
ya I mumble - you're just in time
would your people approve of your gentile attitudes
ah it's all political mumbo jumbo now
memories of the holocaust are fading replaced by
neo-jew pretension
we are what we pretend to have been
and put out an attitude of self-righteous
apprehension
and it serves us well because we have become the
eternal victims
so joshua where do you fit in
i don't know - somewhere between a schnitzel and a
bagel
us non-practising jews are lost
but still you have your tradition and your community
still supports you
you're right

we basically have it all - tradition and freedom
ha ha he laughs
I laugh too
the irony
I'm ordering pizza
extra ham for you joshua
you know I eat anything man
I order 4 large pizzas
get me a vegetarian pink says
ok are you vegetarian
no
josh gets a beer and pulls up a kitchen chair
what's with this labbats blue
johnny's favourite
ok then
I know you like that mexican piss
it's the best
johnny pipes up - shit that's not even beer- it's not
even piss
josh laughs

you painting anything josh asks
ya I just started
lets see he says and heads into the studio
hell it looks like a disaster with this one
ya I just went crazy and now it's time to fix it
interesting
love your stuff
my uncle abe is looking for something
for what room

his study he's just got a picture of the flood hanging
there now
oh ya a friendly reminder of what a benevolent god
you guys have
he wants to come and see you
right on I'm sure he has boxes of cash
boxes - more like truckloads
sounds like my kind of guy
we wander back into the living room
pink is gone
hey where did the chick go
don't know johnny says
she just up and left
that's the way she works
who is she
don't know
the pizza gets here and we eat
it's a happy time with my friends
wonder what happened to pink
we leave half the vegetarian and good thing
3 hours later pink staggers in grabs another beer and
the box of pizza
we make a spot for her on the couch and let her
settle in
she doesn't say a word

gotta go johnny says and he's gone
josh leaves too and it's just me and pink and frank
sitting on the couch watching a movie called the
book of eli

it's a good one
pink is really into it she's talking and laughing and
even crying
the movies over and pink goes and has a bath
I wander in cause I have to pee
she doesn't even look
frank says see you and he's gone
I go back to my painting and work on it for an hour
and head for bed
pink is fast asleep
what a night
I reflect on the day and on the friends I have
I'm a lucky guy I think
just think if I locked my door - knock knock all the
time and what a nuisance
you can be too safe and shut out everything
some languish behind their gates too scared of
everything
I guess that's me too
hiding in my condo - haven't been out on the street
in 2 years
I love to castigate everyone else
love to complain
love to find fault
hate to admit I'm a loser but I am
I am a loser and a racist and a bigot and prejudiced
and to top it all off - a bad artist
if anything I wish I was a gifted artist
I do it for a living and I suck
I hate that

thank god for alfredo and gudrun
without them I am nothing
don't even know what art is anymore
I never pay attention to any other artist
it would make me crazy
got enough of my own wacky ideas
I have to only follow my crooked path
a child - immature
I may paint but it's not really art at all
it's nonsense and it depresses me
I never hang up one of my own paintings
don't want that garbage in my condo
my walls are white and bare - not even a calendar
I turn and fall asleep

chapter five

the phone rings
hello
lido how are you
gudrun fine fine nice to hear from you
I'm coming tomorrow to see you
fantastic
everything will be wonderful see you then
bye aufwiedersehn
without a sales agent an artist is nothing unless
they're a picasso
I'm still waiting for my big break
not holding my breath
my undisciplined unfocused careless sojourn here on
earth does not lend itself to rewards
if gudrun had not taken pity on me I'd be dead
and I have nothing for her this time but she never

judges me
never berates or scolds me
the woman is a saint
never puts me down or belittles me
never puts pressure on to produce
this woman is from god
someone to help me survive
I thank god every day for her and alfredo

pink is gone
hi kitty
I sit on the couch and she sits on my lap
she wants to play and bites me
I get her feather on a stick and play with her
she jumps high trying to get the feather
so funny
kitty are you so funny
we play for a long time
she finally wanders off and eats
I go and have a bath
life is a strange journey
love took me for a ride so many times
always it ended in disaster
I'm jaded
it's all such a masquerade and I always get a bad
costume
I'm always switching it up
find yourself the teacher said to us
what does that mean
I looked here and there and everywhere

reading this and that and everything
trying this and that and everything
I paint
write poetry
make music
dress this way and then that way
trying this hairstyle and then that
I don't know what the hell is going on anymore
I give up
can't find out who I am
I am everything
when I'm with so and so I am one thing
when I'm with another I am another thing
what a chameleon - changing on the fly
doubt and indecision guide me as I crash and crash
and crash
bruised and wounded and nursing a serious case of
self pity I stagger
becoming an outcast
not fitting in anywhere and that is why I stay in my
room
let the world come to me for I am a nothing
I give up

the bathroom door opens and it's gudrun
hey
lido I'm here
I'll be right out
she goes out and I hop out and dry off
I hug her and she kisses me full on the mouth

dam gudrun you get more beautiful every time I see
you
she smiles and laughs at me
lido how are you
you're looking good
I'm struggling a bit but finding my way
she walks into the studio - very interesting
ya you know repainting like usual
I see some good things here
are you ready to sell the red triangles she asks
referring to a painting I did last year
sometimes I hold onto a painting because it's grown
on me
ya I say
good I have a buyer
she makes a call - rufus you can buy the triangles
ya ya good will ship it out today
the canvass if already off the stretcher bars
I go and roll it up for Gudrun
how much
3500.00 - good price
she writes me a cheque
gudrun is astute and honest and the money is always
number one
got to go baby she says smiling and kisses me
love you lido
love you more gudrun
love you most
ha ha
at least I got money - dam I got a good price for that

painting but I feel the loss
that one was at least respectable

I lay down
1750.00 is my share and I don't begrudge gudruns
half
she is my conduit to the world
that's a lot of money
money is everything
money buys it all including love
try love without money - the chick will be leaving
soon without it
good looks get you only so far
why are so many hot girls with ugly guys
it's one of two things - big dick or lots of money
well - almost
sometimes it appears that true love is there
unbalanced forces at play
designers of chemical concoctions

dam it's quiet today
everyone is gone
I go to paint
turning on the bose - simon and garfunkle - sounds
of silence
I paint and as I paint I dance
going into a trance
the world disappears
where is god and what is god
so many gods

the spirits fly all around me as they jostle for
position
each trying to influence the outcome of the painting
a spiritual battle is on
take this
and that
should I paint here or there and what colour
use the spatula or a brush
type of brush
or just throw some paint
I sit back and look
then paint again
on and on into the night
finally I fall asleep on my chair and jerk awake then
go to bed
it is well
it is well with my soul - at least for now

funny that you should say that
it's really a hilarious sideshow
something taking place below heaven and above hell
as if
maybe the crows know
I just think that isabella could have decided the
location
wanting it and needing it or declaring it to be
who is the decider - the arbiter
the judges have the power
forget the will of the people
elected but powerless

appointed and the final word
manipulation of want and desire and spreading it on
thick
see - but maybe if there is a decision to think about
it
consider the evidence
what evidence
it's a vacuum and when the singer decided to jump
off the stage
the audience rose to their feet and applauded
would god applaud the rebellion
a question left unanswered but addressed piecemeal
in all the holy scripture
another slash of red
scratched off with a piece of wire

waves of despair rock my inner man
who is that inner man
a strange voice calling
what
special ears required to hear the sounds of ghosts
apparitions submerged in a crust of doubt
there are rules to follow
there are customs that cannot be broken
there are consequences for rebellion
did we not all learn this in school
as we sat spellbound and fearful in our desks
eyes on the schoolmaster
hoping to be able to catch on
I hated being stupid

I don't understand
you don't understand
dummy
go stand in the corner until you're ready to be smart
okay now what's the answer
don't know
go to the office
smart ass eh
hold out your hand
ten times with the strap on each hand
humiliation and pain and suffering
the bullies struck again
now can you tell us the answer
why are you skipping school
go to school and learn and try to fit in
the terror grows as the abuse grows
and still I didn't understand
oh ya we'll beat some sense into this kid
I move my brush on the canvass

my life has been a freefall without focus and without
a destination in mind
I was broken so long ago
oh please
quit being a baby and hoist yourself up by the
bootstraps
they have taunted and exhorted and threatened and
castigated
I've responded and then given up
now I just drift

you need to make a decision
it's a choice you make like being gay
we'll give you medicine and counselling
you'll come around just wait and see
your abnormality will fade away
you will be normal and like girls again
give us a chance
there was really no closet - I was always bisexual
I liked it all and I felt guilty
I still feel guilty
oh you bad sinner
you are deserving of eternal damnation
yes god I know but I can't help myself
yes you can
don't give in to temptation
give your life to god
say no to the devil and accept the blood of jesus
he will heal you of any of your same sex cravings and
you will be free and whole
it's a choice they preach from all the street corners
everything is a choice
I looked for those bootstraps and all I felt were
paintbrushes so I painted
can't stop now - I'm addicted
I did not choose to paint
as I was free falling I grabbed some brushes and
paints and that was it
silly me
what's wrong with me anyways
something is wrong because I don't fit in with

regular society
but - I have friends
mostly disfunctional like me staggering along life's
highway picking up junk and bottles along the way
and now I find comfort in my disfunction
sorry preacher
sorry teacher
sorry society

but I'm not happy
I am conflicted
and I fear happiness because right after happiness
comes sadness and depression
that's the way it is
it's almost as if I'm content to be sad with occasional
spurts of joy
rain and then a little sun
I am vancouver and vancouver is me

chapter six

I clean up the kitchen
move on to the bathroom
sweep all the floors
do some laundry
I lay down on the couch and fall asleep
I wake up with kitty pressed against my chest
what a precious little soul
I shift and she meows and stands up
I hug and kiss her and hold her on my lap
what's up little cat
you're the best
her motor is going a mile a minute
I pick her up and carry her with me as I walk out on
the deck
my flowers are still flowering and some of my

tomatoes are ripe
I put kitty down and water them
she sniffs the flowers and eats some of the grass I
have planted beside the flowers
I go back inside and put more food in kitty's bowl
and give her fresh water
then back out and sit down on one of the chairs on
the balcony
what a view looking over english bay dotted with
tankers and sailboats
the ocean is so beautiful

I hear someone come in
pink saunters on to the deck and sits down on a chair
hey
how are you
okay
you got plants out here
ya some tomatoes and some flowers
pink and white and purple
what are they called
don't know alice planted them
who's alice
just a woman that used to live here
was she your girlfriend
sort of
did you have sex
every now and then
oh
is she coming back

I think so
how long has she been gone
about 4 months
no word
no word
pink lights up and offers me one
I take it and she throws me her lighter
I light up and throw it back
I shouldn't smoke but I love it so much
we sit on the deck and smoke and look out over the
water
kitty comes and rubs against pink
she picks her up and pets her
we're like a normal happy family out here
hey pink you want some Kentucky Fried Chicken
ya
you want to go pick it up
okay
I tell her what to get and where it is and give her
money and she's gone
I make some mashed potatoes and some corn
she's back in twenty and we eat out on the deck
dam this chicken is good
even pink is smiling
she throws some meat to kitty
she eats it - even kitty knows it's good
while we're eating pink stands up - beer
I nod
we're still drinking labbats blue the best beer in the
world

you like the beer pink
it's alright
why do you call me pink
because you had pink panties on the first time I saw
you
oh

is your bose portable
ya
pink goes and gets it
she scrolls through the music on the iPod
david bowie
she adjusts the volume up
this girl doesn't need to ask questions she figures it
all out herself
now we're grooving I say
she glances at me as if to say - what are you a dufus
she's one of the chosen ones - a golden girl
one of those girls at school that were so beautiful
and cool she reduced all the boys to fools
all those rules still apply except I have had sex with
this one and that would never have happened to the
geek I was in school
why are some people so naturally cool
is it their natural sexuality
cool people are always sexy and uncool ones like me
unsexy
it's a law
I had no friends in school except if you consider a
couple of really low life's

I tried and cried and couldn't figure it out
I was ugly homely and was forced to wear hand me
downs that didn't fit
looking back I can't believe the clothes I wore in
school
what an immigrant
what an outcast
it was really sad

I go and get another beer for pink and myself
I'm feeling good
the beer buzz is kicking in
contentment sweeps over me like a disease
watch out boy - trouble is brewing while you're
getting drunk
and the gods are going to punish you
sinful human wretch
confess your sins
backslider turning your back on morals and god
should be reading your bible instead and doing good
works
should be witnessing to pink
get her soul saved so she doesn't go to hell
someday you will fry
then you will cry
and you will try
to escape but
the angels will keep you in
and the eternal flames will lick your balls as you
scream in pain

torture for ever and ever
amen

I shake my head to get rid of the voices
pink looks at me
something wrong
no just thinking about hell and eternal damnation
oh
are you saved pink
was once but now I'm an atheist
oh
you're really an atheist
ya how about you
agnostic
oh
pink we're a bunch of godless sinners getting drunk
on this deck
yep
are you worried about hell
no it's a fairytale
ya most likely
we keep on drinking
I go and get us another beer each
I'm feeling really good now
and bold
pink you want to fool around
ok
we go to the bed and start to fool around but pink
falls asleep
I lay back down and fall asleep too

waking up I feel groggy
I look at the clock and it's 10:00 in the morning
there is no trace of pink
I go to the bathroom
hi kitty
kitty rubs against me
I fill her bowl which is almost empty and give her
fresh water
I clean her litter
kitty wants to play
I sit at the couch and she jumps on me and bites me
I turn her on her back
she scratches and bites and then runs away and
sneaks up on me pouncing on my hand
we play for some time
I get up and make some breakfast - cream of wheat
and toast
I eat and watch the news
more refugees coming to the country
what a disaster with isis
someone fucked up big time
my phone rings and it's frank - hey lido need some
beer
frank we always need beer-what kind of a question is
that
you got a good deal or something
ya my brother in law got a whole shitload of no-name
beer we can have 20 dozen for like half price
it's 11% alcohol
no-name must be shitty beer but what the hell bring

it over
alright see you in a couple hours
okay bro
good thing I have another fridge in the storage room
probably the only good thing about that beer is it's
high alcoholic content

the painting has come some way now
I managed to find a new path
I turn on the bose
now we got bob dylan playing
I get lost in my art world again
I mix some colours - a little dab here some there
on and on
as I paint I think about my life
so many wasted years where I coasted along and
accomplished nothing at all
so many stupid things I did like stealing money and
getting caught
at 14 I was a juvenile delinquent for stealing 86.00
from a service station
why
I made my mom so sad
but that was it for stealing
after that I said never again
but the damage was done
the trust was interrupted
to hurt my mother was to stab a knife deep inside
myself and it always comes back to stab me again and
again

oh I've been forgiven but I can't forget
dam teenage years of stupidity and confusion
restless always so restless and the endless yearning
feeling trapped and wanting to get out and expand
and fly
my father died when I was 5
I always miss him
a hollow spot in my life that I can never fill
I loved him so much and I feel him all the time
I love you daddy
I miss you daddy
I pine for my father
the deep pain it crushes me
I sit down on my chair look at my painting
I want my daddy
I throw a bottle of paint at the painting and scream
I want my dad
can you hear me
bring him back
but I know he's not coming
dam
someday though we'll get together - I know

chapter seven

I have a barbecue on the deck and take out some
frozen patties and put them on the grill
I take out some frozen bread unthaw it and a little
ketchup raw slice of onion
slice of tomato dijon mustard corn relish lettuce and
mayonnaise on top
the hamburgers are good
no beer today just water
I eat outside
kitty comes and checks out the food
I give her bits of the hamburger
she eats a few pieces and then wanders away to her
own food
she doesn't eat too much people food and that's a
good thing

I wonder where alice is
I've lost track how long she's been gone but it must
be 4 months now
she ate breakfast one day and said see you later and I
never heard from her again
but she's done this before
I've known her for 5 years and she's unpredictable
born in taiwan she like me lost her dad at an early age
she came to canada after high school and went to
emily carr
graduated after 4 years and worked as a barista and
painted
she was pretty good and gudrun took her on and her
paintings sold regularly
every now and then she would go back to taiwan to
see her mother and she'd stay from 3 months to 6
months
but I never had her mother's phone number so I
couldn't call
she isn't on facebook either so I don't know
I finally filed a missing persons report - what was I
to do - well johnny did
I checked with some of her friends but no one knows
where she is
I think she's in taiwan
really she's very strange
she used to come over all the time and every now and
then we'd have sex but like 2 times a year - so weird
she was rooming with some friends and then a year
ago she moved in with me

she didn't bring much just a blanket, a pillow, her
personal stuff and paint supplies
then after 6 months she was gone
I'm worried but can't do anything
when she comes back I'm going to give her supreme
shit
dam what is it with people
where is the communication
no respect for other's feelings
we all affect each other
we need each other
alice where are you
god
the uncertainty kills me
those question marks
the not knowing

I clean the grill and take the dishes inside and load
the dishwasher
I wipe the counter and put the food away
I hate messes
it's not that I'm a clean freak but I like things
relatively clean
I am civilized after all
with barbarians all around me

my life is a boring mess
a monotonous and uneventful existence
go to bed - get up - eat - drink - piss - shit - paint
etc.

this is hell on earth
I am the goldfish
we all are the goldfish
round and round we goes
what's the purpose no one knows
and we duplicate ourselves
who are then also sentenced to this boredom
why bother
why try
we make beautiful ceramic bowls and others take
them and drop them on the ground
all broken now
all that work in vain
with empty hands we stand looking upon our
creation which lies in pieces at our feet
and the destroyer laughs in our faces
anger fills our frame
we turn away in sadness
we lack the courage to punish the perpetrator
we shrink and cower
where is the power
to stand up and face the intruders
why do we wilt like flowers in the midday sun
and like them we fade away - our beauty fleeting

I go inside and lay down on the futon
no music no t.v.
sick of all the noise
silence snickers sarcastically
it systematically dismantles the abstract illusions

as internal forces transcend and vanquish all enemies
of abstract mythology
wrap it up hugo
erase your silly nonsensical observations regarding
the fall of man
stand on the bench and proclaim your derision
our humanity will not stand for it
stubbornly defending its territory lest the critics gain
a foothold
and dictate the direction our art will take

the tension is palpable
a generalized preoccupation transcending ideas that
conform
and thrive in a sterilized environment
where collusion between the avantgarde and the
literalists is disturbing the peace
rip out those pages that history invented
throw them to the spiritual warriors that parade on
the outskirts of decency
where humanity trades in sophistication for barbaric
individualism
I put my hands over my ears
I can't stand it anymore
too many voices
and opinions
crying for a place
how to interpret these philosophical dilemmas on the
canvass
torn apart my soul screams for clarity

but chaos is the order of the day
weary and worn I succumb to sleep
with thoughts clashing and echoing
small wonder some take their lives
it's just too much

waking up is an event
what will I discover on the other side of dreamland
has there been an invasion - a redecorating
kitty is curled up beside my head
she turns and looks at me and gives a faint meow
I give her a pat - nice kitty
she purrs
I look around - not another soul's in sight and it's
dark outside
it's 7:00 p.m.
I turn over and keep on sleeping
again I wake up and this time the t.v. is on
the jew is sitting there eating something
josh what are you eating
hey lido - chinese food want some
sure
there are a bunch of containers on the kitchen
counter
chow mein and beef and broccoli and sweet and sour
pork
I take a little of each and sit back down on the futon
what's up man
I scored tickets to the canucks game tomorrow night
you could come if you weren't such a boo

oh ya maybe I'll come
you're welcome
let me think about it
how many you got
4
holy smokes

I love hockey
the violence and the fights
the pure energy and fast action
I'm a man of peace - why do I like the violence
I should abhor it - be repulsed by it
a contradiction
there is too much violence in society as we give in to
baser instincts and lose control
but in hockey the violence is controlled
did you see how civilized the players look in their
suits
did you see them shake hands after a playoff series
they do good deeds in the cities they play in
young people look up to them and admire them
ya I know they shouldn't admire the violence
I have mixed feelings
I hear you
but dam it I like hockey - I am Canadian
we are taming the game down slowly
give us some time

who am I fooling josh I won't go
I get such bad panic attacks when I go out

just the thought is making me clench my fists
I need help - counselling and treatment and maybe
drugs
but I don't want the drugs - they take the edge off
and I will lose who I am
and most likely won't be able to paint anymore
no I must fight it on my own terms
I don't trust doctors and they're all so arrogant and
overbearing and think they know everything
but we got the internet and we know they know jack
I'd trust a naturalist doctor sooner than a regular one

I know a natural doctor
she'd even come and see you here
really she'd come here
I could do that
in my environment where I'm in control and she can't
make me do anything and I can kick her out if I want
to
can you give me her number
don't have it with me but I'll text it to you tomorrow
her name is Rachel
thanks
that's cool
a visiting doctor - that's my style
and I won't feel as intimidated because she's a woman
men can be such jerks with their out of control egos
okay I'm sexist
I'm more comfortable with women

no beer left in the fridge
oh it's in the other fridge
josh walks to the fridge in the storage room and
looks inside
what's this - no-name beer
ya I got it cheap
it's got a high alcoholic content
oh ya
what's it like
not too good
well let's give it a shot
you want one
nah had too many the other day
you won't drink it - it must be bad
no no it's not that bad
he opens one up and takes a swig and screws up his
face
h-m-m he remarks - interesting
I laugh
some guys are just too kind to say bad things
maybe next time we'll have some of that mexican beer
I'll believe that when I see it
I laugh
what the heck I say and get myself a beer
I open it up and take a drink - o-o-oh
josh watches and laughs
very interesting
we both laugh

chapter eight

josh and I are watching the canucks play the calgary
flames
in the end we lose and we are both bummed
another beer my friend
have to now
I get two beers
so lido what's with pink - she still around
ya she comes and goes
don't know who she is or what she does
I don't know how people can live like that
I know
how's the job going
I love it but it has its challenges
the money's good and I love people
I would be useless

basically I don't like people much
you'd surprise yourself
oh no my friend I can't pretend
josh laughs
being a nurse was never on my radar
I thought it was a job for women but now of course
I'm enlightened
ya till my father died I never thought about it but his
care was so bad it made me want to do it
is it still bad
by and large yes it's the culture
new nurses come in full of energy and enthusiasm
and they get hammered down by the status quo and
bad attitudes
I'm fighting it man and that's the hard part of my
job
I hear you
glad it ain't me
but I'm not complaining - great money and flexible
hours
well lido my friend got to go
have to get some sleep before my next shift
thanks for coming
see you bud
ya brother
and with that josh is gone

I stare around at the empty room
alone again - naturally just like the song
hey kitty what's up

the little cat is curled up on the futon with nary a
care in the world
wonder what goes on in that little head
no language to guide them
how does the thinking go
it blows my mind
the complexity of everything
and this all evolved from nothing
and by accident
accidental accumulation of sophistication
can't accept that but I'm no scientist
what do I stand on
what undergirds my conclusions
without proof everything is open ended
don't have the facts to reach conclusions
I dream
and theorize
and guess
are we political beings
discarded after an interspace referendum
thrown upon the earth to blend music with art and
philosophy
muttering mindless mumblings
inventing and reshaping a picture of what was
combining canvas and paint and strips of leather
interpreting signs and wonders
casting our vision inward
looking for clues
then dancing upon our creations
and separating meaning from intellectualism

a slice of heaven interspersed with modern
architecture
sits upon the shoulders of the elected
those ambassadors of misunderstood misgivings
sorry you and you
and you
fluctuations in the natural order of things made me
confused and therefore
what I said and did was not the same
forgive me and forget and vote for me again
and again
and again
oh sir could you please move over and make room for
me at the trough
oh so sorry come right in and please allow me to kiss
your ass
thank you so much
a patron yes
the honour exhausts me but it is all mine
oh no it's mine
I insist
really
well then let's just sit and talk and reason together
like equals
what was that I just said
sorry can't hear you

I had me a mama and a daddy once
they looked after me even though I was a dunce

the good lord above put me in their care
and my mama stroked my auburn hair

my daddy was an artist and he taught me how to
paint
my mama was a nurse and I thought she was a saint
my daddy up and died when I was five
and every day I wish that he was still alive

when I was twenty-one my mama went too
I really didn't know what I was gonna do

death defies all of our intentions and has no respect
for who we are
he takes and we
stagger in a stupor of disbelief
reaching out longing hands and crawling on our
hands and knees
begging for the return
of all we held so dear
but he laughs mercilessly as he dares us to test his
power
the end the end - he shouts
it's all I have
it's all I need
it's all I want

the door opens and in walks pink
I walk to her and hug her
she hugs me back

what
just thinking about my parents
oh
she touches my cheek and goes to the bathroom
I am so happy to see her
I was lonely for her
she seems so strong
so silent
so secure in who she is
wonder what her story is
someday she might share but I won't ask
don't want to piss her off
in time
all in good time
if she sticks around
and if she sticks around what will happen when alice
comes back
is this the beginning of a harem
am I to be a polygamist of sorts
don't want to be
relationships are too hard and it's no wonder people
separate and leave and get mad
and the kids suffer the most - dam
oh sorry junior mommy and daddy are splitting up
what
let's pack
huh
we're moving to Laredo
where
it's a beautiful place

you'll love it
sure

pink walks out of the washroom stark naked and
opens the fridge door
no beer
in the other fridge
pink goes to the storage room and gets a beer
she looks at me
no
she sits beside me on the futon and grabs the clicker
I'm going to bed pink
she nods
I climb into bed
kitty jumps on the bed and lays down beside my head
I pet her - hi kitty such a good girl

the sun is streaming through the blinds when I wake
up
I look at my radio clock - 10:00
pink is lying on her back naked as before
what a body so slim and yet so powerful
I go to the bathroom
kitty is meowing at me
she's eaten all her food so I fill her bowl up and
change her water and then change the litter
a cat is so little work one might as well think of it as
no work at all
and you get so much in return - a loyal and happy
little friend who will never hurt you

I go back to bed
I have no will power to stay up
I have become very lazy and undisciplined
can I even respect myself at all
what have I become
what would my mama think of me
what would my daddy think of me
they would be disgusted that's for sure
I don't care - actually I do but whatever

chapter nine

I wake up
I'm thinking about the dream I just had
someone was in a dark forest with me and we were
walking along
when suddenly a head without a body appeared in
front of us bobbing along
and talking
hi it said can I walk with you
I thought to myself - you can't walk cause you don't
have feet
ya you can come along but what makes you move
I'm a spirit he said I don't need feet
and so we walked along with the head bobbing beside
us in the darkness
we were lost

I asked the head - do you know where we are
no he replied I'm lost
I didn't know spirits could be lost
apparently yes he said
I thought - this is a dumb spirit
I thought spirits were smart and superior
and that was the end of the dream - very stupid and
very short
I shake my head and get up
pink is still lying exactly as before and the time is
1:00 p.m.

I poach a couple of eggs
I want to create something but my painting depresses
me
I sit down at the table in my studio and sketch
lost in my world of fantasy I lose track of everything
after some time I get up
somehow without me noticing pink has left
silent like a night prowler
she is a night prowler I think
a mystical spirit
maybe she's a reincarnated warrior from a bygone age
lost in our world
an old old soul full of the wisdom of the ancients

I go on the deck and water my plants
kitty comes out and meows
I pick her up
kitty kitty how are you

I stroke her head and under her chin
she purrs
I put her down and she runs around
I go back in and check her food and water
foods good I change the water
I go back in and turn on the t.v.
my man steve harvey is on - I love that show
what a funny goofy guy
he wears all those suits
family feud was never ever this racy and I bet the
ratings are the best too
the phone rings - it's gudrun
hey
she asks how I am and then tells me that the guy who
bought the red triangles wants to know if I can do
another one to compliment it
wow I reply of course I can
I'll finish what I've got and get on it
great says gudrun love you most
ha ha love you most too
I'm a terrible painter on demand guy but that
painting is easy
it has only knife work and I like that
well a little pick me up for today
I'll take down the painting I have on the go now and
work on it in the future
I want money so I'm going to start on that requested
painting right away

I go to the studio and take down the painting

now I need two 48" by 48" stretched canvasses
I don't want to take the time to stretch my own
I call johnny - hey can you pick me up some
canvasses
he says he'll be over in a couple of hours
great
johnny the ex-junkie is mr. dependable
tattoos up the ying yang scars all over his face a sour
demeanour and living on welfare he doesn't fit in
with society but fits perfectly in with me
he's my main lifeline to the world
now I have to think how I will construct this
painting
I can't duplicate the first one - they have to
compliment somehow
I grab some of the magazines from johnny and page
through them
I also look through some of my sketch journals
in these I paste all kinds of pictures from magazines
and sketch out all types of nonsense in an effort to
find something new and fresh and interesting

the phone rings - it's gudrun
hi Lido I'm sending alfredo over to help you with
your vision
right on I reply
ok bye
bye
gudrun already knows I need help and she's right
better get ready to go on a binder for three days or

so
it's party time coming up
johnny's going to be happy - he loves alfredo and
when he's here he hangs around the majority of the
time
we need food and some different beer - no-name beer
won't do for alfredo
it's going to take an investment in booze and food to
complete this painting
I'm excited
I caution myself - don't get too hopeful or happy or
trouble will come
reign in the joy and channel it to the work at hand
I always paint better when I'm drunk
sad commentary on me I think
got to get loose
have to let the inhibitions go
need to wander out to the dark side and peer into
mysteries
push back the curtain and see what the freaks have to
offer
insights into spiritual worlds that revolve and
interact within each other
casting aside my trepidation and with cautious
courage charge into hell
deflecting all the pitchforks with a devil may care
attitude
I am invincible
I am the greatest
I am ready

of course I'm never quite ready
but I pull the wool over my eyes
it's the only way

I go into the studio and put on some music and sit
down in my chair
jumping jack flash is playing
looking into space I wonder
why am I a basket case
where are my angels with their angel wipes
an angel with a mask peers through the window
poor poor human don't be sad
stand on your pedestal and testify
think about all the righteous victims
glory in the beauty of their suffering
ok then where is the substitute
who is singing
the choir of tormented lepers joins in at the chorus
unhealed nonbelievers
but I heard it plainly I really did
george carlin said it
all the madmen laughed as they frolicked in the
midnight sun
all that fun
those nameless and shameless debutants carousing
and posing

the yellow bus is driving to Damascus
paul was there
blinded by the light

those jesus moments
seems like many of us have them
put on your red-striped jeans and prance like a
maniac

who is that pressing their nose against the stained
glass windows
looking for gold or pigeons or pirates
a reckless meandering in a dangerous place
where victims don't cry
where vagabonds carry guns
please - open up your ears
listen to the music
pounding
caressing
stroking

her lips were slightly parted and puckered
sitting on the stoop
a daydream away from yesterday
and all the maidens were dancing provocatively
the lying went on
without interruption
and then there was Romeo and Juliette
first Shakespeare - then Knoftler
a reinterpretation to catch up
some were napping and missed it all
too busy counting prayer beads
or sticking needles into the veins of their necks
going down

losing the battle and then - BANG

lucky again
surviving again
notes climbing the scales promising so much

on the streets a gang of poets wielding slingshots and
pulling down their pants
the police playing violins and jumping the puddles
the strings were calling
and humpty was falling
again

how did the crow ever get drunk
some glad morning
Jesus is everywhere that son of a god
let the congregation rise

if not triangles maybe circles
I need some beer
I need Alfredo
I need food
I don't even know where to start
painting is stupid
it's dumb
it's senseless
what purpose does it serve and what is the meaning
of it
purposelessness
depressing

chapter ten

I shake my head and just then someone comes into
the suite
hey
ya Johnny
but it's not Johnny it's Frank
Frank what's up
not much thought I'd stop by for a beer
right on brother
I get him a no-name
here's your beer brother
Frank opens it up and takes a swig - good stuff
you like it
ya
thanks again for getting me all that beer
you never had one before

nope this is the first
right on
I think to myself - goes to show everyone's got a
different sense of taste
well man we got lots of that
don't I know it
we laugh
we sit on the futon and watch t.v.

I met Frank about 5 years ago when I was still up and
about
met him at the penthouse on Seymour a strip joint
the penthouse is a landmark in Vancouver
we used to go upstairs in the good old days
you could eat and drink in an intimate setting with
the strippers dancing right in front of you
met Frank there one afternoon and we became
drinking buddies
after the upstairs shut down around 6 or 7 or 8 we
went out on the Town
never got home till noon the next day
been friends ever since
Frank is a jazz musician - a dam fine drummer
works the local scene but also goes out on tour
Lido I'm gonna order some pizza
right on
he calls
while he's calling the door opens and Alfredo
staggers in already looped
I hug him he kisses me back

Lido I'm here let's party he yells
I laugh and put my arm around him
buddy it's been too long
will you have a beer or a beer
I think a beer
I fetch him a no-name
he looks at it - no-name - are you kidding
oh well he says and cheers and down she goes
he grimaces - oh buddy it's good I'm here things
must change
I hear you got some painting to do
ya commissioned no less
congrats buddy it's amazing
ya I'm happy but I don't know what to do
let's see what you got
he wanders to the studio
nothing new here
ya I'm waiting for Johnny to come and get me some
stretched canvass
oh Johnny my buddy
he'll be happy you're here
oh we're going to party I can feel it
yes we are and in the middle of all that I better get
some paint on some canvass
you will my friend you will I've got faith in you
we've been here before
I laugh we've been here many times and you rescued
me every time
Alfredo you are an angel
no no no Lido I'm the devil and I've come to distort

your sense of reality
it's what I need ha ha

hey Frankie how you been buddy
good good Alfredo
what pizza you order
Bella's
very good my friend very good
these guys been here a long time
they know pizza
ya they do I interject

Alfredo sits down on the futon with his beer and
yawns
well Lido we have some serious shit to do this
weekend
and don't think I'm going to let you slack off
I want to see some real painting going on
and not some pathetic crap either
reach down into your soul and fetch something we
can feel
I look at Alfredo and laugh,
yes master I will do my best
oh don't think I'm kidding
I'm going to take off my belt if I have to and
administer a good old fashioned licking if I have to
I'm shaking in my boots
you better do

the door opens and in pops Johnny with a couple of

4X4 stretched canvasses
hey he mumbles shuffling to the studio
hey Johnny-boy Alfredo shouts
Johnny kicks him as he walks by grinning
he goes to the storage closet and gets a beer.
here's to you asshole he tells Alfredo as they clink
bottles together
it's been awhile

there's a knock on the door
come in
the pizza boy walks in with 5 large pizzas
what the hell Frank you ordered 5 fucken pizzas
Alfredo yells
oh ya Frank replies this is serious business here
you da man Frankie you da man
Frank pulls out his wallet but Alfredo stops him put
that away Frankie this is on me
he pulls out a wad of cash pays the guy and gives him
a big tip
thanks man
never mind we'll need you again real soon
and the pizza guy is gone
holy shit I say this is serious pizza
better get eating Frank admonishes
the room falls silent as we start eating

Johnny settles in on the chair while the rest of us
Alfredo Frank and me sit on the futon
we're having a great time and I look around and

marvel at the scene
these are my friends brought together by who knows
what
alfredo is part of the art scene so that's his
connection and he's become the star attraction
he's got energy for 4 and is full of joy and laughter
no wonder Gudrun keeps him around
we need guys like him - he brightens up the world

I sink comfortably into my seat and watch the scene
around me
I feel like an onlooker listening to the chatter with a
smile on my face
these are my people
this is my family
without them I die
oh crazy world of wonder and chaos and tragedy
you toss us around like clothes in a dryer
aimlessly we rise and fall
touching each other
interwoven
prisoners within walls of steel and concrete searching
for warmth and friendship
protecting ourselves and weaving our own armour
stay away and come close
don't touch and feel my pain
caress my face and fuck off

the beer is flowing and the pizza is being eaten
and the voices

louder and louder
I sneak off into my studio and set up two canvasses
maybe one of them will work out
I page through some of the magazines Johnny
brought me as I sit in my chair
I got nothing so I squeeze some paints out on my
piece of glass
I take a palette knife and randomly apply paint to
both canvasses
if ever there was proof that I'm a lousy painter it's
here
aimless and without any creative instinct I push on
I am discouraged and depressed about my work
what would Picasso do I ask myself
he at least had natural ability and a work ethic
what am I
what do I bring to art
Nothing

I keep on
I scrape and swear and apply and wipe off
what I want to do is take the canvasses down and piss
on them
so I take them down and piss on them
the piss runs all over them and down on the floor
I get a pail and sponge and mop it up
as I'm mopping up the piss Alfredo finally
discovering that I'm gone comes into the studio
what's that smell he asks as he wrinkles his nose
piss I say

what the fuck
oh ya Alfredo I pissed all over my paintings
Alfredo goes into the next room
guys guys Lido has lost his mind he's pissed all over
his art
everyone comes running into the room and gazes
with horror on my paintings which are laying on
the floor with colours running together and piss
dripping off the edge
Johnny burst out laughing and falls down so great is
his humour
Frank stares in disbelief
Alfredo stands in front of me and looks deep into my
eyes with tears in his eyes
he proclaims very solemnly - Lido today you became
a real artist
I respect this
I respect you
you're doing it all for art
you've hit the bottom and here you will find what art
is telling you to do
he grabs me and hugs me an honour to know you
buddy
I will love you forever
you are a Picasso no doubt
I look on in disbelief not believing what I have done
and surprised at the reponse.

as we're standing there in walks pink
she walks up to the paintings and asks - piss

I nod my head
she walks out and Alfredo asks- who is the queen
I don't know she walked in one day and she's at home
here now
wow
is she your new girlfriend
nope
is she available
who knows
the paintings are forgotten and we follow Alfredo
into the main room
pink is sitting on the recliner with a beer and pizza
and smoking a cigarette
she's watching t.v.
Alfredo just stands there and stares at her
finally she looks at him - what
oh he mumbles sheepishly totally transfixed by her
he shuffles over and holds out his hand - my names
Alfredo
she disregards him and keeps on watching t.v.
Alfredo doesn't know what to do so he goes and sits
down on the futon while the rest of us laugh at him
Pink glares at us with an icy stare

I love this woman what a bitch and so cold
it's sexy as hell
and I know it's not an act - this is pink in all her
glory
now there's no conversation and everyone is just
drinking and eating and watching t.v.

Alfredo looks at me and raises his eyebrows
he takes out a pack of smokes and lights up
clearly he's baffled by this one
I go back to my piss and the paintings and put them
back on their easils
I take a cloth and wipe the sides
as I stand back and survey the damage I realize that
they look good
the piss has had a transforming effect
I go and bum a smoke from Alfredo and sit in my
chair and look at the paintings
what to do next
what about some conformity to the red triangle
painting?
fuck it for today
I go and join the rest of this bunch of lunatics and
misfits
pink is gone
I look in the bedroom and she is sleeping with the
cat cuddled up beside her head

chapter eleven

at 1:00 in the morning Frank leaves
10 minutes later Johnny goes
it's just Alfredo and me
we chat for awhile
Alfredo I'm going to bed you got the futon man
I love this futon
me too
I get him a blanket and some pillows
he lays down and is asleep immediately
wow this guy was wasted
I go to the bathroom brush my teeth and go to bed

dam that sun
what's the time
Pink is gone and the time is 11:00
I get up Alfredo is sound asleep snoring like a bear

I laugh
Kitty is scampering around playing with her toy
mouse
she meows at me
I give her food and water and clean her litter
I clean up the mess from last night and wash the
dishes
I go out and water my plants and sit down
it's a beautiful morning and the seagulls are crying
the ocean stretches out in a blue paradise - heaven on
earth
I go and make some oatmeal porridge
I go back outside
the fall air is a little nippy but what a beautiful
September morning
I'm glad I didn't drink too much
no hangover for me
now as for Alfredo he's going to be sore
I better make him some coffee he needs his coffee in
the morning
I go inside and he's rubbing his eyes - Lido I need
some coffee
I know man I'm going to make some
don't bother I'm going to Starbucks
with that he's off to the bathroom and takes a shower
5 minutes later he's out the door with a see ya bro
I know Alfredo
there won't be many words for awhile
he's all talked out and hurtin
but never complains - dude is a real mensch - a

trooper

I finish cleaning up the mess from last night
then back into the studio
I sit for awhile staring at my two canvasses
I put on the music - Simon and Garfunkle
the music brings back the melancholy that I'm
looking for
I mix some paint and get back to my painting
time goes by and I'm lost in my meditation
in my mind the forces of heaven are fighting for
supremacy
Jesus is calling all angels to arms
they assemble on a great plain in heaven all on white
horses with Michael the archangel at the head
the trumpet blows and its onward ride
the slap on the back knocks me back into reality
bro you doing alright
oh ya
I'll be back in a couple of hours
see you man
and with that Alfredo's gone again
I sit on my chair and contemplate the essence of my
work
what is it
art is so stupid we do some shit on a canvass or
whatever and then stare at it
someone buys it hangs it on a wall and stares at it
we are a fucked up humanity

I go back to bed
I need some sweet dreams
where is a compass I can borrow so I can
find a harbour to anchor my ship
why am I so insecure
I am a painter that's what I do for a living
people buy my work
I make a living creating art so I must be an artist
but I know I'm a lousy artist
is there really such a thing
I am what I am - I should stop questioning it all
I used to paint still life and portraits and landscapes
but
I've evolved into an abstract painter
what am I to do
do I have to place myself in a box
if anything I'm Jackson Pollock without the
personality or talent
I guess an abstract expressionist in some form
whatever
or did I just get tired and lazy and now I just live and
paint undisciplined
a chaotic existence
like a bum...

why ask why at all
the turbulence of naked artistry
a blowing wind caught in its own downdraft and
suspending
reason along with natural inclinations

dampened by societies demands
the lighting of the fire - a ritual consecrated by The
Doors
organ music rousing ancient spirits
the vapour rises from the lakes of contradictions
clashing and slashing and mashing
maybe this or maybe that and how about

I think about Alice
where is she
I'm troubled
maybe she really is dead
her mother does not know my phone number
maybe she does but doesn't care enough to call
it's all up in the air
unresolved
Alice where are you
please god look after Alice and send her back to me
I at least want to know she's alive and well
I drift off to sleep

the kitty is licking my face and meowing
hi kitty
I pet her and she purrs
I get up no food I fill up her bowl
she has lots of water
kitty goes to her food bowl and eats
the door opens and in pops Johnny
hey man what's up
hey Lido guess what

what
I saw Alice last night
really
I'm wide awake now
wow
ya I was at the Safeway on Davie close to Denman
standing in line when someone prods me from
behind
and there's Alice smiling with a basket of food
hey she says how you been
I just about shit my pants and say good where u been
I've been here for a couple of months living on bute
I went to Hong Kong for awhile and then came back
Lido's been worried about you why didn't you call
him
I thought you were his girlfriend
no I never was his girlfriend I was just living there
for awhile
well he's been worried sick about you
he worries too much
can you call him at least
maybe
are you still painting
no I'm working for Telus as a tech
oh
with that I paid for my stuff and said bye and left
I can't believe it she doesn't even care
that hurts man
ya but now you know
now I know

some people are so cruel
I go and get a beer for Johnny and me
we go outside and drink
people are strange Johnny
I don't get it
ya Johnny replies
people are strange

we're sitting there and pink walks out onto the deck
she goes back and gets a beer
hey pink you remember Alice Johnny says
ya
so he relates his experience with her
pink raises her eyebrows and keeps on drinking
what's the time Johnny
6:00
where's Alfredo
he went for Starbucks at noon I think
is he coming back or is he pulling an Alice
me and Johnny laugh
oh he'll be back

my phone rings
hi Gudrun
Gudrun tells me that she had to get Alfredo to do
some stuff for her
he won't be back
okay see you soon
there you go Johnny Alfredo as been summoned by
Gudrun

party's over
fuck that it's just begun
you guys feel like Chinese
sure
johnny's out the door and me and Pink keep on
drinking as the darkness closes in
pink goes back inside and turns on the t.v.
I go in and go to the studio
sitting in my chair I process the news about alice
I slowly start playing around with my paintings

lost in this world I twirl like a dancer
heeding not the words of the sages
love is a lost art
something to wonder about
a noncommittal act of revenge or war
I sip my beer
I poke at my paintings
I feel sorry for myself and allow helplessness to
overshadow me
a victim I am again
weak and needy and poor of spirit
blessed are the poor for theirs is the kingdom of
heaven
heaven I long for thee
here on earth I am a pilgrim
wandering aimlessly along this crooked path where
demons and trolls lurk
to punish me
to hurt me

to ensure I pay the price for all my indiscretions

pink walks into the studio and stares at the paintings
come on she says and takes my hand leading me to
the bedroom
she shuts the door
she strips down to her panties - pink and frilly
I undress and we make love
cigarette
ya
two lonely souls lying on their backs smoking
cigarettes
a cliche
there's a knock on the door
foods here
we get up dress and leave the room
johnnys got a lot of Chinese food
hey John think you're feeding an army
nobody gonna end this party lets go
and we're all in
Pink and I get some food and another beer and go sit
on the futon
Johnny's on the recliner
Pink clicks thought the channels and me and Johnny
shoot the breeze
pink finds a movie - true lies
pink I love that movie
me too chimes in Johnny
Pink nods her head
we eat and drink

it's a great night
to hell with love
to hell with responsible living
let's party and let the world be damned

chapter twelve

I wake up and it's dark
I look at the time - 8:00 a.m.
no sign of Pink
I get up and look outside and it's raining cats and
dogs
I go to the bathroom then take a couple of aspirins
got a hangover
back to bed
can't believe Alice
just can't process her rejection
took me by surprise
I don't know anything anymore
who is who
ain't no morning light here - darkness inside and out
kitty snuggles up to me and purrs

I pet her

the masks our faces hold
hiding
and how like armour
we peer out as frightened
probing
doubting
longing for the caress and daring
dreaming
pausing then rushing headlong into
embrace
the nearness intoxicating as breathless
we pull back
scared but again
intimacy seduces and
as catapulted into the warmth we trust
then recoil
shock at the rejection and wondering
confused we stagger

the music drones on and on
what does it matter anyways
when love spits in your face and
all you knew was wrong
and the living becomes a meaningless sojourn
why not the noose
why not the slashed wrists
why not a bullet to the brain

I turn and turn
my restlessness leaves me angry and bitter
always it ends so bad
always it ends
always love turns her head and spits in my face again
and again
then who am I and why am I
why must I so defeated be here
where sunbeams shine and moonbeams dance
and joy should be a friend
and I get the girl and she stays to the end
just like in the movies
and happy ever after

I drift off
waking up I cautiously look beside me wondering
I catch my breath
yes she lies beside me
an angel
the fallen soldier revived by an angel of mercy
I look at her face
so very beautiful and so serene
her blonde hair caressing a proud and noble
countenance
I reach out to touch her but draw back
afraid to invade her space
she is not betrothed to me
she is not my lady
she's just passing through and I
an unworthy spectator here in this arena of despair

I dare not dream of us together
forever
tis not a dream for losers like me
destined to a life of loneliness and chaos and
melancholy
we may look
we may touch
but only for a moment
I drift off
dam the sun
dam the light
noon
pinks gone
I get up and feed kitty and get her water
she pushes against me and meows
I pick her up and pet her as I walk over to the
window
there are whitecaps in English bay today
it's beautiful
blue sky and clouds competing
kitty bites my hand
I put her down and she goes to eat
I walk to the studio and sit down
the paintings are coming along - one more than the
other
I put on my apron and squeeze out some paint
I turn on the Bose - the Doors are on
today I'm at peace with my painting
I've moved past the uncertainty
past my battles with the canvass

I paint and scratch and flick
finally a vision is appearing
it's coming to life
I witness again the birth of a piece of art
so much struggle and doubt
and after the self-doubt and
despair - triumph at last
I sit down
done
it's a sweet moment when I finally give up and admit
that the painting has vanquished me
you win again I shout at the painting
you've conquered me again
I am the loser
you are the winner
but I'm a happy and content loser
I sign my name
I hear the door open and some banging and cursing

I walk into the main area as pink is rolling a large
suitcase into the apartment
she heads to the bedroom and mumbles hi
I look on as she rearranges my clothes in the closet
any spare hangers
oh ya I'll get them
I go to the storage closet and get a bag of hangers
thanks
I walk dumbfounded to the kitchen and make some
scrambled eggs
pink is moving in I mouth silently to myself

Alice did the same thing
they don't ask
they just move in uninvited
I sit at the table and eat the eggs and listen to pink
after an hour or so she appears and heads out the
door
see you later
see you

I go to the bedroom to survey the damage
I've managed to retain 1/4 of
the closet space
she's also commandeered 4 of the the 6 shelves
squishing my t-shirts and shorts together in a
disorderly way
her things are neatly folded and arranged on the
remaining 4 shelves
purses are hanging from one of my hooks
dresses and pants and blouses are hanging jauntily on
the pipe with my stuff squished together
she put her suitcase in the storage room beside the
fridge

I look in my dresser
she's taken the top two drawers for underwear and
sweaters
she had a lot of stuff in that suitcase
where did she live before
some nerve these women have
they don't ask

they just move in
I am truly a doormat
do I even exist at all
I shake my head and go to the studio
one down and one to go

chapter thirteen

this first of the two attempts at one commissioned
painting I will call "The Womb"
it started looking like a womb after the piss
I built on that theme as I went along
it worked out
I actually like it
now to finish the other one
the pressure is on
I sit down and observe
time for a beer
I get a beer
the door opens and it's josh
beer
ya
back into the storage room

I grab a bag of chips while I'm there
come into the studio man
he follows me
what do you think
he looks at them silently and nods his head
this ones finished I call it the womb
I can see that
I like it
now the other one I think it needs some collage
we walk out to the deck
what a day
I know
just finished my shift tired as hell
you look it man
lay down on the futon if you want
na it's okay
I tell him about Alice and Pink
we laugh
oh my god

Josh changes his mind and lays down on the couch as
we talk
after a couple of minutes he's asleep
I feel tired and go to bed
pink has moved in
what does that mean
it doesn't feel real at all
it's a dream I know it and soon I will wake up
I really don't want the commitment of a girlfriend
and I like to live alone

who am I fooling I'm never alone
there's always someone in here
so maybe I don't mind
I groan within myself
perhaps the purple hairy rabbit will come and rescue
me
I see him there at the cave still dancing
and above him the e-string is being stretched from
tree to tree

old mythologies are congregating at the entrance
as plato - tied up - conjures up
recipes for proper introspection
including a special section on the coming christ

who is that old drummer smacking the skins
and mixing in a good old-fashioned batch of
hallucinations
give god the glory glory
fits and sticks
and a john that kicks
the pretenders into a corner where they can be
consoled by greedy
industrialists who still smell of fascist dogma
those underminers of pure judaism
reinterpreters of dogmatic principles that stood so
straight
as winds of change swept through the land
purple green and blue
throw your cuss words into the stew

naked sally right on cue
doing what she do
as you think you're through
being the latest version of you

high-stepping Nazis are smiling
waving their green cards
proudly
let the wheels go round
the temperature rises and
what's that
I can't hear you
oh I know he's tearing up the gospel
at the auditorium
she is tearing off her clothes
together again
shredded in the basket
yesterday's bright futures
the undertaker with a bet
and of course the revival and renewal
of vows where black curtains
illuminating
dark eyes peering so intently from
where
wherefore
whereof
I saw the masked intruder take out a sausage and
laying down on broken glass the dancing nymphs
tickets and concerts walking hand in hand and
commenting

a political rhapsody listening to the latest news
pounding against the surf
where are those protest proposals they left on the
desk
too much love
the understanding broke the back of protocol
tinkle the keys

a definition that gasps
hate that spews as love hews
into the rock the statue
are those principles founded on precedence or
made up as the imbecile drove his bicycle
on the sidewalk
why the decomposition of the corpses at midnight
on an off chance that
only a consolation prize would be offered
the lurking of men in bathrooms preceded by a court
order
thou shalt not do such a thing
a penalty of five farthings
protests and more protests
she dares to say that thou dost protest too much
who's slouching
crouching
making the bad music as eaten
alive by snakes in the pit
a no-mans land defined by guitar riffs
an interjected solace and coming down the steps
a maestro

turning over I yawn
the darkness caresses my eyes
life can go to hell
what purpose I
an endless battle of the wits
survival a boring ritual of nonsensical actions
dam that pink
everything is ruined
and dam myself for being so weak
so pathetic
manliness I never had
I should jump from my balcony
end it all
purposelessness and uselessness
I sigh
and the night claims me again

chapter fourteen

moving in
it ain't no sin
even so - bring out a bottle of gin
and ask me - can I win

I wake up scared to look
slowly I turn
nobody there
I get up and look around
not a soul in sight
a question lingers in the air
where

kitty looks up at me with a quizzical look
I pick her up and carry her to bed

she curls up
I fall back asleep

I wake up to the sound of the T.V.
pink is watching a movie and I get up
hi
hi
it feels a little awkward and I see the question in
pinks face
pulp fiction is playing and Mia and Vince are dancing
I start to dance twisting and prancing
finally I'm jumping all over the room my eyes closed
in meditation
to my surprise pink is dancing beside me
now I'm travolta and pink is thurman
I grab her and pull her close
I guide her to the bedroom and it's on

am I in a trance
I truly love the mademoiselle
somethings changed
you never can tell
the irony
pink actually looks like Mia
who am I - Pierre or
Vince
it's such a sweet confusion as delirious and crazy I
fumble about

I searched all around the world

well - in my little secluded world
for love
have I found it

I'm letting go and
falling I grab pinks ass
sweet Jesus help me now
her lips find mine and we enter no mans land
the fount of love has opened

I am a servant
a slave to love
playing as the names are called out on the p.a. system
roll call revisited
where spectators are left
speechless
the feeding of the five thousand was a miracle and
this

the ghastly images projected on
ancient ruins
a heartfelt scream issued
yet

none will be left standing as this kingdom
rises
to heaven and then

I should have been wearing tails and a top hat
and all those musicians on clouds of joy

a faded desire as the years
old faded ripped up jeans
Fashion
take a look
please

the answers are being rewritten
fame and fortune chasing a chopped up estate

can crazy warnings save the prophet
okay then
the happiness offered as a ransom
as in the vale the harlots
played into the hands of the wise men
three they were
with myrrh and frankincense and gold

the mist
the gods will surely strike
as wheels go round
and round

one we are
filled with songs and psalms
unknown and stoned we flail about in this symphony
a rejected lovers land
blisters and wounds so deep
as the cold cold wind blows
and the soul tries to make sense of all the mysteries

we pray in this garden
oh lord may thy spirit fill us
here in this bastion of creation where love is random
where arrows fly about
and lonely mornings at the river become forgotten

still she kisses and her hands so spiritual and strong
caress my broken frame
as tears fall
with hands lifted to heaven

the ufo was identified
names attached
sobriety guaranteed
why have all the promises been broken
as hopeless the lover stood
waiting for hotdogs

who died to save your soul
who played you that rock and roll
who scored the winning goal
who sat upon the skinny pole

all those plastic moments
we were searching for peace even as we were ready to
die
still
the guitar combines with the violin as
the preacher
reads revelation and lays down on the floor

trample me
spit upon me

the dancer moves silently on the dance floor
as blades of truth
rise
up through the floor boards

she is a righteous rocker
and her music appeals to me
even as
her voice breaks
windows

the fans are giddy with joy
vanquished
the jets fly

and the seven angels blew their trumpets
as God stood at the throne lifting his hands
unleashing the forces of heaven
was it good for you
I smile weakly as she brushes my tears away